Gone

The Missing Years of Bjorn Esterday

Book 06

Dolphin Express

2031

Wynter Sommers

Wynter Sommers

This work is registered with the UK Copyright Service, in accordance with the Copyright, Designs and Patents Act 1988 All rights reserved 284718038 for

GONE: The Missing Years of Bjorn Esterday

Published by Pure Force Enterprises, Inc.
California, USA
Since 2002

INGRAM

INGRAM® Distribution

DEDICATION

To those who feel strongly about truth, justice, and the integrity of America; your honorable actions make us proud.

To those who wonder if their daily choices matter; your small decisions impact generations to come.

To those everyday people who don't think they have what it takes; your perseverance and strive for the extraordinary, makes the impossible a reality.

To those who have failed; know you will make it and tomorrow will be better.

Your dreams today become our future tomorrow.
Thank you for everything you do.

Bjorn Esterday
Was Not Born Yesterday
Series

Firebrand (15 Volumes+Conversation Station Book)
Edges (9 Stories +Conversation Station Book)
Gone (24 Stories + Conversation Station Book +
Longfellow Journal for 26 books in Gone set)

Bjorn EDGES Series
EDGES Book 1-Swift Encounter
EDGES Book 2-Rousing Attack
EDGES Book 3-One Foot Under
EDGES Book 4-Earthshake
EDGES Book 5-Broken String
EDGES Book 6-Key Witness
EDGES Book 7-Who is She?
EDGES Book 8-Vanish
EDGES Book 9-Chase or Die

Bjorn Series Alternate Reading Plan

<table>
<tr><td>1st</td><td>Edges Book 1</td><td>25th</td><td>Gone Book 11</td></tr>
</table>

1st   Edges Book 1

1ˢᵗ	Edges Book 1	25ᵗʰ	Gone Book 11
2ⁿᵈ	Edges Book 2	26ᵗʰ	Firebrand Vol 10
3ʳᵈ	Gone Book 1	27ᵗʰ	Gone Book 12
4ᵗʰ	Firebrand Vol 1	28ᵗʰ	Gone Book 13
5ᵗʰ	Edges Book 3	29ᵗʰ	Firebrand Vol 11
6ᵗʰ	Firebrand Vol 2	30ᵗʰ	Gone Book 14
7ᵗʰ	Gone Book 2	31ˢᵗ	Gone Book 15
8ᵗʰ	Gone Book 3	32ⁿᵈ	Firebrand Vol 12
9ᵗʰ	Firebrand Vol 3	33ʳᵈ	Gone Book 16
10ᵗʰ	Gone Book 4	34ᵗʰ	Gone Book 17
11ᵗʰ	Firebrand Vol 4	35ᵗʰ	Firebrand Vol 13
12ᵗʰ	Gone Book 5	36ᵗʰ	Gone Book 18
13ᵗʰ	Gone Book 6	37ᵗʰ	Gone Book 19
14ᵗʰ	Gone Book 25- *Longfellow's Journal*	38ᵗʰ	Edges Book 5
15ᵗʰ	Edges Book 4	39th	Edges Book 6
16ᵗʰ	Firebrand Vol 5	40ᵗʰ	Gone Book 20
17ᵗʰ	Gone Book 7	41ˢᵗ	Gone Book 21
18ᵗʰ	Firebrand Vol 6	42ⁿᵈ	Edges Book 7
19ᵗʰ	Gone Book 8	43ʳᵈ	Gone Book 22
20ᵗʰ	Firebrand Vol 7	44ᵗʰ	Firebrand Vol 14
21ˢᵗ	Gone Book 9	45ᵗʰ	Firebrand Vol15 (End)
22ⁿᵈ	Firebrand Vol 8	46ᵗʰ	Edges Book 8
23ʳᵈ	Gone Book 10	47ᵗʰ	Edges Book 9(End)
24ᵗʰ	Firebrand Vol 9	48ᵗʰ	Gone Book 23
		49ᵗʰ	Gone Book 24(End)

ACKNOWLEDGMENTS

We acknowledge those who actively build peace. We acknowledge all the selfless talent which contributed to creating meaningful tokens of consideration and sharing. We acknowledge that every person has a daily choice of right or wrong... and we thank you for choosing the right, good, honorable path filled with integrity because that is the difficult and brave path. Small choices today become lasting monuments of loving hope tomorrow.

HOW TO INTERPRET THE CHAPTER TITLES

How to read this book: The title has two numbers. The number on the left is the chapter order in this book. The number on the right of "chapter" is the consecutive continuous chapter in the entire series. The number in parentheses is the year and the rest is a chapter title, sometimes sharing which location the chapter takes place.

For example, below is a chapter which appears in GONE Book #03. It is chapter 6, but GONE continuous saga chapter 13. The action takes place in the year 2030 in the location of Brio in the Gardens. The year is in parenthesis.

6 CHAPTER 13: (2030) BRIO: GARDENS

CONTENTS

0 Settings IX

    Locations IX

    Characters X

0 PREFACE 1

1 CHAPTER 24: (2031) COURTLY CITY: FANCY RESTARUANT: SARAH AND MARK DATE 4

2 CHAPTER 25: (2031) COURTLY CITY: HIGH SCHOOL BREAK ROOM & CAFÉ: SARAH AND THE WILBUR DATE 25

3 CHAPTER 26: (2031) COURTLY CITY: LIBRARY: SARAH INTRODUCES GEORGIA TO LIBRARY AND MRS. LIBRIS AND WATSON 44

4 CHAPTER 27: (2031) ISLAND: SHORE: BJORN ON LAND 54

5 CHAPTER 28: (2031) ISLAND: SHORE: BJORN WAKES UP AFTER ISLAND NAP & GETS SLOBBERED 62

6 CHAPTER 29: (2031) ISLAND: VILLAGE: LONGFELLOW APOLOGIZES TO THE LOCAL VILLAGE MAN 71

7 CHAPTER: What Just Happened? 85

8 Did You Know 87

9 Vocabulary 88

0 Locations and Characters

Locations

- **AromaX**: City of fragrance & fashion
- **Courtly City**: City of solar & other technical products. Bjorn Esterday and Sarah Paradise live here.
- **Brio**: Underwater village
- **Maastricht** a place in the Netherlands where Longfellow has a winery

Characters

- **Dr. Lou Pole Linden**: Research assistant to Otto Mattick in the AromaX labs
- **Otto Mattick**: The Mattick family is an elite class in the city of AromaX
- **Topliner**: The relative of Otto
- **Georgia Peach**: Fellow teacher at Sarah Paradise's school.
- **Sarah Paradise**: Teacher and met Bjorn Esterday in EDGES series
- **Bjorn Esterday**: Reporter at the Daily Memo in Courtly City and with a mistaken identity now a resident at Brio.
- **Zor**: Manager of Brio
- **Watson**: Charismatic motivational speaker
- **Tres**: Works with Watson
- **Mrs. Libris** is the librarian in the last Courtly City library
- **Pat Seeds** Gardener in Brio and managed Bjorn during his stay in Brio
- **Longfellow** - partners with Warren -Former resident of AromaX, now resides here and training recruits and working at a winery
- **Warren Piece** -partners with Longfellow. Former resident of AromaX, now resides here and training recruits and working at a winery

0 PREFACE

Guilt. Pride.

How do you combat feelings of guilt when an innocent person gives you what is precious to them and you feel undeserving? Did Bjorn's actions cause the downfall of Brio? Must he survive or will he grapple with survivor's guilt, constantly wondering why he has a chance at life while others have been cheated?

What of Sarah? She is skilled, talented, and kind, yet seems to be blamed for the actions of others, even well meaning coworkers. Should she maintain her integrity realizing some may not feel guilty about how they blame her? Should she change and "play dirty pool" and call them out for their misdeeds? How do you handle a besmirched reputation where you are genuinely innocent?

And you know who is guilty.

What deliberate decisions will Bjorn make to justify his second chance? What choices will Sarah make when confronted by one offense after another? If "grace" is defined as granting a second chance to those who offend you, how do you prevent yourself from being a "doormat"?

What will Bjorn do to make his future count? What will Sarah do to earn respect and clear her name? What is the price of succumbing to guilt or your pride?

Last time, in the year 2031, Longfellow tested the Comm range on the Island.

Warren Piece and the dogs rescued him after he fell into a deep hole. Longfellow later wanted to test his crew and gadgets, especially the Burst technology.

Meanwhile, Bjorn escapes from the Brio Pod and finds aquatic salvation resulting from the unexpected and regular kindness of Pat Seeds' consistent effort to feed the aquatic life living around the Brio bubble. Dolphins take an exhausted Bjorn and show him...land.

Back in 2030, we see that Georgia has surprised Sarah, who is trying to thaw a chicken for dinner, by showing up at Sarah's condo and convincing her to go out.

In 2031, Georgia convinces Sarah to go on a blind date with Mark.

1 CHAPTER 24: (2031) COURTLY CITY: FANCY RESTARUANT: SARAH AND MARK DATE

Checking the address Georgia had given to Sarah earlier at school, Sarah walked along the Boulevard until she found the restaurant where she was to meet Mark, the blind date Georgia had arranged.

She stood in front of the huge sophisticated black iridescent doors. The door-frame itself displayed an array of rainbow colors rolling rhythmically along its surface. She reached for the shiny crystal handle, but then stepped back as the doors slowly swung open.

A man and woman, holding hands, almost collided with her as they exited, but swung around her and hailed a wheeled vehicle now pulling up at the curb. The man sported an elegant navy blue jacket over his white silk shirt. His companion wore a bright red dress with her raven hair swept up.

Sarah looked down at her bland beige colors, which matched the drab environment of school. Sarah wondered if her simple wardrobe would be fancy enough to walk inside the imposing restaurant building.

Sarah had put on her AromaX lipstick, using the flat shiny cap as a mirror to make sure the color was on straight.

She smoothed her hair and gave her collar a couple of tugs to see if she needed a spritz of fragrance. She shrugged and reasoned on a first date she wouldn't get that close to this Mark guy, anyway, so assuming she passed muster she walked in.

She didn't even change her shoes and still had her backpack with her.

Mark recognized Sarah from Georgia's description and stood up graciously, holding out the chair for her to be seated.

"Hi, I'm Sarah, Georgia's friend. I came straight from work," Sarah said brightly as she curtsied.

Mark stepped in to hug her. Surprised, Sarah, with her elbows now firmly pinned down, tapped him lightly on the back with the palm of the one hand.

"I was worried since I was waiting for quite a while. You should have called," Mark complained, concerned.

"Um," Sarah said while they were still standing, "Well, I don't have a comm and...I don't know how to contact you even if I did have a comm...soooo..."

"Well, next time, Baby," Mark said. "Please, sit."

Sarah was about to sit across from him in the booth, but he pulled her to sit right next to him. They both faced a wall now, since the table was at the end of a long row of diners.

Mark continued with, "Oh, your hair looks exciting all windblown like that."

Uncertain how to respond, Sarah said, "Um, I need to brush it, but.." She shrugged.

"Nice lipstick."

Sarah gave a shy smile as she recalled how the lipstick had come in a rolled up copy of the Daily Memo... Bjorn...

"So, Georgia tells me you are a school teacher at her school," Mark started, as he snapped his fingers for the waitress.

"Uh. Yes. And the profession you are in...?" Sarah asked.

"Marketing," he smirked, "where image is everything. Others judge me based on who they might see me hosting. Just as people will never believe you are only a teacher when they see you with me."

Then he sniffed and reached into his pocket for a tissue to wipe his nose.

"Oh, do you have a cold? The kids in class always have some germ to share," Sarah forced a grin.

"Don't you get sick from sick kids in the classroom?" he asked Sarah as, again, he snapped impatiently for the bus boy, pointed to his nose, then indicated a pile of napkins stacked at the busboy station, where utensils were stored.

The busboy reluctantly brought over a stack of paper napkins for Mark to use, depositing them at the end of the table. He didn't clean away the crumpled ones Mark was collecting into a tiny pyramid.

Sarah explained, "When I first started working with the younger kids, I was sick all the time, but I think I built up an immunity to student germs, or something. I rarely get ill nowadays."

Sarah smiled as she looked around. "I've never been here, before. How do you like their food? I mean do you have a favorite dish you want to order?"

"I already placed my order." Mark leaned back. "The filet mignon." He took a gulp of his wine, draining the glass and refilling it with the bottle next to him.

"You like your wine," Sarah kept her smile frozen, determined to give this date a chance.

"It's Maastricht wine. Imported. The best," Mark replied expecting Sarah to be impressed. "You are a teacher, so probably want a light and fruity white, like the Riesling or a Rivaner. I have ordered a Cuvée to start, and a Pinot Noir for my meal."

"I don't really drink so I don't know one wine from another," Sarah apologized.

Mark took a fresh cocktail napkin and blew his nose, adding to the used crumpled pile. "Maastricht is an area far away which makes superb wines." He snorted, muttering to himself, "I have to teach the teacher." He then turned to Sarah and added, "M-double-A. I hear they will soon set up distribution here in Courtly City. As a teacher, I assume you have simple tastes and wouldn't appreciate the quality, anyway."

Sarah replied, reaching deep inside herself for a polite response. This was after all, her friend Georgia's gift to her and she wanted to assume the best of this Mark.

Sarah replied, "I don't really drink wine."

The waitress arrived.

Sarah scanned the menu, then smiled,

"That sounds yummy with a baked potato. Or maybe I'll have the cordon bleu...one of those." She folded her menu and was about to speak when the waitress made eye contact with her, trying to signal with a faint frown, but Mark gestured indicating he's got this. Then, he reached for another cocktail napkin and spoke as he wiped his nose

"Oh. Are you our waitress? I thought I had the other gal..."

"Your original waitress asked me to take care of you for the rest of the evening. What can I get for you?" the waitress replied.

Mark started, "My friend here will have the salad. Not the dinner size, the side appetizer size....and water..."

Mark smiled at the waitress then added, "I like how you did your hair like that."

The waitress nodded, ignoring the comment, and left.

Mark had used up his tiny stack of napkins and snapped at the busboy again for replacements. Once the busboy saw Mark, a split- second expression of distress crossed his face. Then the busboy pretended he didn't see Mark's gesture and headed toward the kitchen.

Sarah leaned in and spoke just above a whisper, "Oh... um...thank you for ordering...that was thoughtful, but I thought I would order the steak or chicken since you ordered the filet mignon. Um, would you mind if I asked you why did you order a tiny appetizer side salad for me instead?" Sarah smiled trying to understand.

"You know you'll be real hot when you lose fifteen pounds," Mark quipped, winked at her, then excused himself for a moment.

Mark sauntered over to the waitress as Sarah sat there wondering what to do next.

She overheard some of what Mark was

saying above the buzz of other dinner guests. The one sentence she could clearly discern was when Mark said "Separate checks" and then a moment later heard the waitress giggle.

Since Sarah was facing the wall, she turned in her seat to see Mark tucking a wisp of the waitress' hair behind the waitress's ear. Then, he seemed to playfully grab her comm and was entering his contact information. The waitress glanced around uncomfortably.

Sarah was about to get up. She had

decided to leave when Mark returned to the table, forcing her to slide in while he took the outside, blocking Sarah's exit.

Now, she was sitting in front of his pyramid of used tissues. She didn't know where to put her hands.

Mark beamed. "So, you are a school teacher. I'm an executive director at our Marketing firm...does that turn you on?" Mark leered, staring deliberately into her eyes, while instinctively tapping one hand out for a fresh cocktail napkin to tend to his running nose.

Sarah leaned back so fast, she bumped her head on the wall behind her.

Not finding a fresh napkin, Mark glanced at the end of the table and reached for a used one, uncrumpled it, and wiped his nose. Then inhaled a snort to clear out the remaining debris in his nostrils.

The busboy came by and deposited a basket of bread rolls on the table.

"Um…turn me on? Does your position at the company turn me on?" Sarah could not find words to say anything else.

She reached for one of the hot rolls in the bread basket at the center of the table. As she reached for one, Mark smiled and pushed the basket away so Sarah could not take a hot buttery freshly baked morsel. Sarah had not eaten all day. She was hungry.

Mark wagged a pointer finger at Sarah winking with his best Casanova-like seductive expression.

"Um. Mark," Sarah started, "maybe I should tell you that as teachers we really only get about 15 minutes for lunch and I had to do some paperwork for a student file, so I didn't get lunch today at all, and I'm awfully hungry."

He moved closer and Sarah's elbow jerked back accidentally knocking a glass of water over, spilling the contents onto the tablecloth.

Sarah, knew that in this caliber of restaurant, the wait staff was to place the napkin on your lap. If you wore black, you'd have a black napkin.

If you wore a light color, a white napkin. Realizing the wait staff was ignoring this table, Sarah reached for the napkin and started to unfold it to sop up the pooling water in the center of the table.

Mark reached over and without breaking eye contact, removed the napkin from Sarah's hand and with a wiggle of his eyebrow, used it to wipe his nose as he spoke.

"We will have to work on cutting down your appetite, little lady, so you can exist on love and air. We all know a woman wants a man to tell her what to do. We'll make you into a refined lady, yet. It will just take some work, my little Pygmalion." He assumed Sarah would interpret this statement as charming.

The meal arrived, presented by five haughty waiters.

Sarah's small salad was artfully done with four leaves of kale and one large crouton in the center branded with the logo of the restaurant.

Two decorative shaved curls of Parmesan cheese sat on either side of the center crouton.

Mark's aromatic dish displayed a large

portion of four filet mignon augmented by garlic herb butter melting on top of each portion.

Every segment of filet was separated by a bacon-wrapped spear of asparagus. The center of the plate contained a small bowl of creamed spinach. The silver cover was removed from a separate plate to reveal an oversized baked potato laden with butter, chives and sour cream, surrounded by a ring of roasted mushrooms and flame broiled zucchini, artfully arranged next to a smaller yam soufflè and Yorkshire pudding.

Mark leaned back to wipe his nose with the cloth napkin he had taken from Sarah. Then, he placed the napkin back on her lap while sliding his hand over Sarah's thigh.

Sarah jerked her leg away as Mark grabbed the breadbasket he had recently pushed out of Sarah's reach. He took a roll, chomping down on it, spewing crumbs all over Sarah.

"I love it when women are svelte, sexy and hungry. You are doing a good job turning me on, Sarah-the-teacher," Mark whispered.

"Huh. That really was not my goal, today," Sarah said. "I just wanted to meet a friend of Georgia's and get a quick bite to eat…because, as I just said, I have not eaten all day, you see…"

Mark replied as if he hadn't heard Sarah speak.

"I know I'm about fifty pounds overweight but, really, it doesn't bother me. I have a personal trainer who keeps me in shape."

"Oh?" Sarah said, incredulous.

"I just can't stand," Mark started with intense emotion, "I just hate to sleep with a lumpy fat chick."

Sarah couldn't resist. "Don't you find that logic somewhat circular? Perhaps even hypocritical?"

"What do you mean?" Mark asked, "I'm being honest and I have standards. That's why I chose this place. I knew a school teacher would do anything to eat here. I mean you couldn't even afford the bread roll."

Sarah replied, "This is the first time we've met. You don't know my preferences."

Mark snorted, wiping his nose with a grin as he explained.

"Well, you are just a school teacher and this is a very nice place. I was being considerate because I figured you couldn't afford either of the dishes you mentioned earlier."

"I couldn't afford...?" Sarah clarified, then paused and returned his smile, as she spoke carefully.

"Your logic, Mark, is hypocritically circular." Sarah explained carefully pronouncing the multi-syllabic word.

She continued, unperturbed, "You're trying to control my meal. Is that your way of indicating a wish to control my life? You certainly have not shown me what a considerate companion you might

be. I won't be rude, since you must feel quite desperately unable to be of any meaningful influence in some vitally important area of your life, but I do not welcome your attitude, nor your treatment. "

"Hey. I'm being considerate. I'm a catch. I asked the waitress for separate checks because I couldn't expect you— on our first meeting—to buy my wine, here. So, you just need to pay for our meals."

"You expected me to pay for your filet mignon?" Sarah asked, blinking.

"See? This is why nice guys like me finish last."

"So, you consider yourself to be a catch? As nice? As considerate?" Sarah stared, her mouth agape, as she couldn't believe how highly he thought of himself.

"I don't believe in that old adage that whoever invites pays," Mark affirmed. "I believe the more you demand a woman do for you, the more control she will give you and the better your life will be. I have to explain to you who is boss in a way your little lady mind can understand, right?"

Sarah replied, "Lessons on manipulating people was not what I had in mind for this evening."

The waitress came over and slid the bill to Sarah for his meal and her uneaten salad.

Then the waitress placed a huge ice cream bowl with nuts, bananas, chocolate syrup and strawberries in front of Mark. The waitress snapped at the busboy to clean up the puddle of water in the center of the table.

Mark wagged his finger at Sarah again.

"I see you have trust issues. When you come home with me tonight you'll see you can trust me in bed." Mark shoved another spoonful of creamed spinach into his mouth, letting a bit of it drip onto his belly, which protruded out from the rest of him like a soft mountain range.

Sarah Paradise looked directly at Mark, and spoke with precision. "Mark, I am not going home with you."

She pushed him back, stood up on the bench, and neatly hopped over him to the floor.

Once he realized she was standing in the aisle, Mark quickly grabbed Sarah's arm with one hand, while jamming food non-stop into his mouth with the other hand.

"Why not?" Mark whined as he drained the bottle on the table into his glass.

He snapped his fingers and pointed.

The sommelier quickly brought over another wine.

"Oh, I knew I would get you jealous when I gave that tight little waitress my contact information. Now you are primed, but you have to wait until I finish my meal. Oh, Sarah, I know you'll be wild in bed tonight. We have such chemistry."

Mark picked up the bill and handed it to Sarah.

"Understand this. Rude, inconsiderate, ill mannered and controlling...it's all a turn off, Mark," she explained and batted away his attempt to, again, present her with the bill. Sarah walked away and said over her shoulder, "I am not paying for any of this and am leaving now."

"Oh, so you want me to go to your place?" Mark seemed genuinely confused.

Sarah sped up walking and did not turn back as she bolted for the door.

"I'll call you..." Mark bellowed with a

full mouth. He chortled to himself, "I've got her hooked."

Sarah walked out the door and reasoned she still had time to grab a burger to take home.

For some reason, she was in the mood for beef.

2 CHAPTER 25: (2031) COURTLY CITY: HIGH SCHOOL BREAK ROOM & CAFÉ: SARAH AND THE WILBUR DATE

Sarah's thoughts were interrupted when Georgia joined Sarah in the Teacher's grey breakroom at Courtly City High School.

The breakroom sink only ran tepid or cold water. Never hot. Sometimes the teachers would donate soap and sometimes they would be without hand soap for a while.

In the dingy concrete school, the brightest thing was Georgia when she strode into the room with a smile and one of her brightly colored outfits, which Sarah could never wear.

"Sugar," Georgia started, "I am so sorry about that little Mark incident. Let me make it up to you. Truly! Wilbur should be...well, not so aggressive. A nice guy."

"Georgia," Sarah replied, "I'm not really ready for another blind date."

Georgia put her hands on her hips.

"Listen. Dating is better than drugs. If it's a bad one, you've got something to chat about with the girls. If it's a good one, we plan for wedding bells."

"Does it have to be one extreme or the other?" Sarah asked looking at the time.

"Our fifteen minute break is almost up. I've got to get back to class. I can't wait for Summer."

"Well, enjoy it while you can since it'll be the last summer you'll have," Georgia quipped.

"What do you mean?" Sarah asked.

Georgia whispered, "Well, I've been seeing this...um... insider..." Sarah recoiled, "You've been dating an administrator?"

"Shhh..." Georgia urged, "I can't have anybody find out. The other guys may get jealous."

"How many men do you juggle at once?" Sarah asked, incredulous.

"Enough to get some good intel! No, it's not official but," Georgia leaned closer and said, "I hear they are going to request we get second jobs during the breaks." She looked around, "...so, I'd advise you find yourself a guy to help pay for a meal every now and then."

"Ugh," Sarah retorted, "Is that your sales pitch for going out with this Wilbur guy?"

Sarah opened the door to the teacher's lounge and started walking with Georgia back to their classrooms.

Georgia replied, "No, my pitch is...you are single and you are not going to meet anybody at work, so why not? Administrators? What have you got to lose? Worst case is he becomes a friend...or a contact for a future job."

As Sarah approached her classroom she glanced at Georgia and asked, "Who is that guy leaning against my classroom door?"

Georgia adopted an innocent expression and replied, "Oh, that... Well, that's Wilbur. He said he'd wait for you since you only have one instruction period left today. Isn't he a gentleman?"

"Why do I get the feeling, Georgia," Sarah commented as Georgia was about to head off to her own class, "that I'm dating the guys you discard?"

Georgia shrugged, "There's no crime in that, is there? The fact is, I'm searching for a special somebody with a certain something. Maybe we can double date one day…I'm just sharing resources…"

Georgia hurried away to her classroom.

Slowly, Sarah approached hers.

The children were already at their seats and this Wilbur stood up as he saw Sarah approach.

"Hi," Sarah said, "I'm Sarah. Georgia told me you might be stopping by."

"I am Wilbur," he said as he gave a short bow.

Sarah observed that he was not fit, yet wore a stretchy shirt, which was a couple of sizes too small, as if he were showing off a well- toned body, which he, obviously, was not.

"Uh," Sarah started, "I will be teaching this class uninterrupted."

Sarah started to walk into her classroom

"I am Wild Boar," Wilbur said firmly.

"Pardon me?" Sarah asked, "Amble white board?"

"No," Wilbur corrected. "Catching a wild boar is tricky. An honor to catch one."

"Good for you," Sarah said as she moved to enter her classroom and close the door.

Wilbur followed and said, "I am named for the catcher of wild boars. Grrrr."

Sarah turned around and looked at him, "Wild boar?"

Wilbur replied, "But you can call me Wilbur. It's faster."

"Sure, um. Wilbur, but I am teaching a class, right now," Sarah explained, "so, I'm going to stand at the front for about an hour. Might we talk later?"

Sarah held her classroom door open

for Wilbur to exit.

"Oh, that is fine," he said as he walked in past her, moving slowly. "I will stand in the room. Shhh."

All Sarah's students stared as Wilbur made his way to the back of the classroom and leaned against a wall when he saw there was no place to sit. After a moment, he slid down against the wall to a seated position on the floor.

With a plastered-on smile, Sarah conducted her class under the watchful eye of Wilbur, who was now sitting motionless on the cold dusty floor in the back of her classroom.

After Sarah dismissed her class for the day, she began packing up her own belongings.

Wilbur slowly approached when the last student left.

"I..." Wilbur started.

"Yes?" Sarah asked.

"There is a café down the street," Wilbur replied. "Let us walk."

Sarah looked around and shrugged. She gathered her backpack and then locked up the room behind them as they exited her classroom.

She took a very silent walk with Wilbur to the café down the street.

Sarah tried to start a conversation.

"So, Georgia hasn't really told me much, Wilbur. Would you like to share anything about yourself?"

"I..." Wilbur responded as if he had explained everything with the one syllable.

"Pardon?" Sarah asked.

They arrived at the café and Wilbur walked in ahead of her, leading Sarah to an empty booth as he repeated, "I..."

"Yes," Sarah replied, "I heard you, but you what? I mean, what did you want to say?"

"You are a teacher," Wilbur replied slowly.

As Sarah slid into the booth, she answered, "Yes. I am and I don't know what you are." She paused and then added, "...you don't use contractions...do you?"

"I would not," Wilbur replied as he stood deciding on which side of the table he should choose to sit.

"Um... Could you explain why?" Sarah asked, looking up at him. She was calmly polite as she would be with any visitor to her schoolroom.

"You are a teacher," Wilbur said as he also slid into the booth, but on Sarah's side, pinning her to the wall with such force, she gasped for breath. This manoeuvre seemed to be a rehearsed pattern with Georgia's former dates.

"Yes. We already went over that… why don't," Sarah emphasized the 'T' in don't and continued, "don't you use contractions?"

"Teachers insist on using the verb 'I', so I will use the word 'I'," Wilbur smiled satisfied, his face but a mere inch or two from Sarah's.

"Pronoun…I," Sarah shook her head. "I'm sorry. I didn't mean to correct. Wouldn't you be more comfortable sitting across from me?"

"No. I good," Wilbur explained happily.

The waitress came over, much to Sarah's relief, and placed two water glasses down with an orange slice floating in each.

"What can I get you?" the waitress asked while chewing gum slowly.

Words tumbled out of Sarah's mouth, but were drowned out by Wilbur, "Two salads with thousand island dressing."

"Um," Sarah held a finger up, "I don't need thousand island dressing."

The waitress asked, "Is Italian all right?"

"Fine," Sarah said shrugging.

"Back in a jiffy," the waitress replied as she turned on her heels. "Ha!" Wilbur burst out, "Jiff! Teachers are down on drugs, right?"

"Jiff is a drug?" Sarah asked.

Wilbur leaned in even closer. "Cocaine."

Sarah tried to scoot back but found she had little room, so sputtered out, "Jiff could be a slang term for coke, but the term 'Jiff' or 'Jiffy' has been around for a few hundred years or so."

Wilbur ignored Sarah's words.

Sarah continued with her lesson, "Back in the 18th century, thieves used the term as slang to mean lightning. Later, chemist Gilbert Newton Lewis wanted to officially define the time it takes light to travel only one centimeter in a vacuum as a 'Jiffy', which is just over 33 picoseconds."

Wilbur's nose crinkled as he said, "Jiffy".

Sarah, not wanting to give him time to form a full sentence peppered him with, "For some computer scientists, a 'Jiffy' is the time it takes for one tick of a timer, which is about 10 milliseconds. Electrical engineers believe alternating currents or the time between AC power cycles was about .02 seconds or twenty milliseconds. But in general, a 'jiffy' is about .01 second. I would assume the waitress simply used Jiffy to mean she'd come back very quickly."

"Hey, you really are a teacher. I thought she was kidding."

Sarah asked, "She? You mean Georgia?"

At that moment, their waitress returned holding two salads.

Wilbur started chomping away almost before the plate was fully resting on the table.

With a mouth full of Thousand Island dressing, and having not yet swallowed, Wilbur leaned toward Sarah and said, "Woooow. I mean it. A true blind date! You really are a teacher."

Sarah nodded politely as she attempted to pick up her fork and reminded Wilbur, "You did meet me at a school, watched me teach a class, and was introduced to me by our mutual friend, also a teacher…"

Suddenly snapping his head from his salad to frown at Sarah, he asked, "Why are you not eating your salad? Do you need positive reinforcement to eat healthy?"

"Eat healthy?" Sarah asked slowly, looking up from her wilted lettuce leaves to unwillingly meet his gaze. She was comfortable with well mannered students.

She was not comfortable with this specimen of one of Georgia's leftovers who also thought so highly of himself that it exhausted her to think of other facts to spew at him just to keep him well behaved. She had noticed a lack of well-mannered, respectful gentlemen around Courtly City and felt she had to reckon with reality and give this Wilbur a chance...but his chance was definitely expiring. Sarah was tired, and in no mood to endure his lack of manners.

Wilbur explained, "Yes. You need to eat more salads. At least that is what Mark told me."

"Mark told you?" Sarah asked, "You know Mark?"

"I am his personal trainer to keep him in shape," Wilbur replied. "He needs to cut down on drinking imported wine."

"You…" Sarah glanced at him up and down and slowly added, "keep Mark in shape?"

Without warning, Wilbur leaned in and gave Sarah a cold, wet, dressing-filled kiss on her neck.

"Hey, teacher," Wilbur started, "Why is dressing called French dressing? I wonder why there is not a salad for every country?"

"I think," Sarah replied hesitantly while trying to find a napkin to wipe off her neck, "French, Greek, Italian, and Asian Sesame dressing exist… I even think there is a Catalina Island dressing, which has Ketchup, red wine vinegar, onions, paprika, Worcestershire sauce…"

"Which country owns the Thousand Islands dressing?" Wilbur asked.

Sarah spoke as if addressing a child…

"I think the wife of a fishing guide created that dressing, and a 1900's movie star loved it. This star stayed in a fancy hotel while her home was being built in the Thousand Islands. The chef added the dressing to his menu and Thousand Island dressing became famous. Um, but, I'm not sure a country can actually own a salad dressing recipe..."

"The Romans own Caesar dressing," Wilbur suggested, "but I think they call themselves Italians today. The Swedes have meatball dressing."

"Do they?" Sarah, struggling to touch her fork, but found it just out of reach since one of her arms was smashed against the wall and the other pinned down by the presence of Wilbur pressed against her.

"Um, Wilbur," Sarah smiled, trying to be polite, "My arm is losing feeling and I can't reach my fork. Could you scoot back a teensy bit?" She spoke as kindly as she could.

"Perfect," Wilbur replied as he inched

back, dropping his fork in his plate with a clatter, then placing one hand on each of Sarah shoulders, twisting her to fully face him as he continued, "Did Georgia tell you I make fashion photographs?"

Sarah replied, "I thought you just said you were a personal trainer…"

"They say I am really good. Do you want to see I sample photos?" Wilbur asked.

"Uh," Sarah exhaled as she quickly snatched up her fork, while it was still within reach and took one bite of lettuce leaf wondering why all her dates had to involve salad.

"Sure," Sarah relented while looking Wilbur up and down, wondering where on his skin-tight outfit Wilbur would have stashed a portfolio to show.

Wilbur pulled out his comm device.

Sarah commented, "I'm saving up to get myself a communication device. They hold so much data...more than the HIB."

Wilbur rested his comm on the table between their salads and turned it on to reveal an image hovering over the device.

He waved his hand and the photographs appeared. Sarah stopped eating and slowly lowered her fork.

The pictures she was now looking at... were of her!

Her walking to her classroom.

Her teaching in her classroom earlier that day.

Her ordering at this café, but the photo was taken from under her chin, a most unflattering angle.

Here was an image of her trying to reach for her fork as one hand was pinned against the wall of the booth right before she asked Wilbur to scoot back... taken not two minutes ago.

Sarah's eyes calmly searched his smug face as she wondered how he could he have taken these surveillance photos without her knowledge.

She hoped Georgia had never told him Sarah's address lest Wilbur decide to plant a hidden camera in her own home.

Bjorn... Bjorn... Sarah thought. Had she merely dreamed him up out of nothing?

"So, what do you think?" Wilbur asked. "Do you feel glamorous, now? I know I am a better catch than Mark. I, right?"

3 CHAPTER 26: (2031) COURTLY CITY: LIBRARY: SARAH INTRODUCES GEORGIA TO LIBRARY AND MRS. LIBRIS AND WATSON

Sarah Paradise and Georgia Peach walked through the doors of Library into a vast room of shelves lined with paper-paged books.

Georgia's mouth dropped. She had never seen so many books displayed, unprotected, to just reach out and touch.

Georgia giggled as she ran her finger along the spines of several volumes. She knew if there were even one such book in in her own city library, the one she had originally come from, it would be on display, under guard, in a transparent case, and mounted in a museum.

Library, a very old building, had more character than the sleek ebony buildings of most of Courtly City. This library architecture seemed to be from before last century and was more inviting. The external construction material was comprised of cold concrete, but Mrs. Libris, the librarian, had planted bright flowers at the base of the wide steps leading up to the entrance.

Mrs. Libris told Sarah, that some Earth Farmer women helped her plant the blooms. The natural stone composite steps and the wood banisters from yesteryear made this place an escape for Sarah. She enjoyed the change of scenery.

Sarah whispered, "This is the last

standing Library I know of. Mrs. Libris told me a wealthy benefactor left a permanent stipend in his will for her to run this place when he died."

Georgia asked, "Can you really find any sort of information here?"

Sarah nodded, "Oh, sure you can. Remember when my computer broke? Well, there's no school budget for tech repairs, so since the system was functionally archaic, Library here had some old manuals. It took me a while, but I not only figured out how to fix mine, I actually built one."

"You did not, Sugar," Georgia poo-poohed.

Sarah walked in and smiled at Mrs. Libris, lowering her voice as she whispered to Georgia, "Yes, I did. See over there? Mrs. Libris had some bits of old computers laying around, so for practice I cobbled that one together. It turns on. May not be a full working computer, but it does turn on."

Mrs. Libris, smiling, joined Sarah and Georgia to ask, "How do you like your new job, Sarah? Been there a while, now, eh?"

"Oh," Sarah shrugged, "This is my coworker, Miss Georgia Peach, Mrs. Libris."

Mrs. Libris gave a short curtsy as Georgia extended a hand.

Mrs. Libris laughed, "Oh, you are originally from out of town aren't you, Georgia.?"

"Why, what makes you say that Mrs. Libris?" Georgia smiled.

Mrs. Libris replied, "In Courtly City, a long time ago, there was quite an outbreak of illness and as a matter of preservation, the wealthy realized they needed to keep their distance from other people. The custom started such that the ladies curtsy and the gentlemen bow instead of touching hands."

"So, there used to be more casual touching and now there is not because our behaviors changed because of this thing which made the citizens sick?"

"That's right," Mrs. Libris affirmed, "Even social romance changed. You could say they decided to not risk getting familiar with so many people. They had to choose if a relationship would be forged before physical contact risked getting somebody sick."

Georgia muttered, "So this sick-thing. It was everywhere? Like an epidemic?"

Sarah added, "I think it was everywhere. A pandemic. Didn't your city get it?"

Mrs. Libris continued, "Pandemic. That's right. Every corporate city was exposed. But, also, Courtly City Culture not only eradicated the source of the illness but they changed their daily customs to avoid future outbreaks. Socially, this even forged our protocols of romantic interaction to determine who will marry whom. You can't just go to some hydration station and meet a stranger and then expect that to be a lasting relationship. They might be an asymptomatic carrier and inadvertently kill off your entire family."

"So, these culture protocols. This started with the upper class?" Georgia winced.

Mrs. Libris explained, "Because the upper classes were keeping their distance from others, yes. Formal greetings, like a bow to greet or say good-bye to somebody, were soon adopted by the masses, the lower classes."

Sarah added, "We always want to copy whoever is famous or wealthy, right?"

Georgia remarked, "Not always. Not if they are not well behaved."

Mrs. Libris surmised, "The people, in my opinion, imitated what they saw worked. The wealthy remained healthy and in power...so the other classes also adopted these daily protocols."

"And other corporate cities?" Georgia asked.

Mrs. Libris thought then said, "Because of Courtly City's alliances, when our formal social protocols kept the illness at bay and allowed us to remain a profitable bossiness force, our allies adopted these customs as their own."

"All of the corporate cities did this?" Georgia asked.

"Those who did not," Mrs. Libris explained, pointing to a book documenting that period of time in Courtly City history, "either perished, went bankrupt, were bought by another corporation, or were so remote that only when we established the safety protocols to remain free of the illness, they had the luxury to revert to those old fashioned business greetings such as touching palms and shaking hands."

"You are quite a cultural detective, Mrs. Libris. In fact, I did move to Courtly City not too long ago, but I love it here."

Georgia smiled, "It's my new home. You are a wealth of information, Mrs. Libris. So glad I met you."

Sarah smiled at Georgia, "See? You learn one thing and can then put the dots together to solve almost any puzzle."

"Agreed," Georgia said looking around.

Mrs. Libris winked, "Come, ladies, tell me what you want to find out about, and I'll direct you to the books you need."

"Well, I come here all the time. So Georgia? Is there anything you want to know more about?"

Georgia smiled, looked up and asked, "What should I learn about...?"

"Is there a puzzle you want solved?" Sarah asked.

Georgia shrugged, "I don't know, Sarah. What perplexes you?"

Sarah replied, "Almost everything."

Georgia prodded, "The Administrators?"

Sarah shook her head, "No. They control my paycheck so I need to tolerate them no matter how many times they change my teaching curriculum."

Georgia asked again, "The Soldier Police?"

Sarah looked up, "Well, since Skipper Courtly put money into redesigning their uniforms, they do look sharper. But, no."

"Um," Georgia tapped a finger to her lips, "Public speakers who have tons of devoted fans?"

"Oh!" Mrs. Libris interjected, "Watson is certainly charismatic."

"Really?" Sarah asked, "You don't see

him as some travelling smooth-talking guy who has the answer to all your problems? You don't see him as a Trust-me-Now-Give-Me-All-Your-Life-Savings-Confidence-Trickster?"

"That's it!" Georgia squealed, "Mrs. Libris, Sarah wants to find out more about Watson. Please, direct us to your bookshelves."

"I thought," Sarah retorted, "You'd be more interested in a book like 'How To Troubleshoot Your Mate'..."

As Mrs. Libris led the way, Georgia replied, "I already own the digital version of HTTYM. How do you think I learned how to get so many fellas?"

4 CHAPTER 27: (2031) ISLAND: SHORE: BJORN ON LAND

Bjorn realized he was lying on his back in the sand. He awoke with the morning sun burning into his eyes. Was he on an island or a mainland?

Gradually, clouds gathered, obscuring the horizon.

Bjorn, aching when he moved, slowly got to his feet to evaluate if his limbs all worked.

Thirsty, hungry and still disoriented, Bjorn stumbled away from the deserted beach and headed inland to see what awaited him, or what food he could forage.

After a long walk, Bjorn came upon a pool of water. He dipped a finger in to see if it was fresh or salty. It seemed fresh. Bjorn, always watchful, scooped up a handful of water, carefully tasted it, and then drank from it until satisfied. He looked around for a cave of some sort, but the entire area seemed flat.

He heard the hum of buzzing bees. Then birds chirping.

"Nature never sounded so good," Bjorn sighed as he slumped back onto his haunches. After a while he mused, "I guess I have to find a place to sleep tonight." He did not know when, or if, he would find civilization. He was simply glad to be on dry land.

Bjorn, feeling very alone, now heard an odd squawking and quacking.

"Huh?" Bjorn wondered as he looked around, then, watchful, stepped toward the sound. When he rounded the corner, he saw ducks flapping about in the tall grasses, a short way from the pond.

Where there are ducks, Bjorn figured, there may be a nest with eggs.

Bjorn plunged into the pond's muddy waters to search the shoreline for eggs.

Every now and then, he would look up and spy a new type of bird. He had never seen so many varieties in his life at Courtly City. Truthfully, he had never seen a bird up close before.

He was awestruck by these displays of feathers.

He had always thought birds tweeted, but these birds honked, quacked, and almost barked. He wondered what the birds ate, and then saw one bird dive for what sounded like a bee. Bjorn wondered then if there was honey in this place.

But how, without any supplies, could he figure out where he was...to find honey, food, or even how to get back to Courtly City.

That first night he slept in the open, on dry grass, under a tree, but with each subsequent night, Bjorn had restless dreams reliving the horrors he imagined he had caused to Brio.

It was difficult for Bjorn to realize he probably would never see Pat Seeds or any of the others again. Guilt clung to him like the honey he sought to eat.

How much longer could he survive? It was time Bjorn trekked around to see if he could find some signs of civilization.

One morning, he got up and realized, by the direction of the sun, that he must have been wandering in circles on the very eastern end of this land. It was time to head west and do some organized exploring.

Slowly, almost reluctantly, Bjorn started to walk. He looked down at himself.

His clothes, what little remained of them, were dirty and undoubtedly unpleasantly aromatic. He felt his chin and noted the beard, which had started to grow. Bjorn rubbed his face, then put his hand in his pocket and felt the HIB.

He pulled out the small device, which Pat Seeds had thrown at him before locking Bjorn into the pod and expelling him to a watery unknown.

Bjorn shook his head as he observed the device and muttered, "Pat Seeds. What is on this Holographic Identification Badge? Why did you give it to me? Why didn't you come with me?"

Bjorn shook the recent memories from his mind with a shudder. Then he walked until he needed to rest. He was not as strong as he once was. He was surviving on grass and roots.

Bjorn had no idea how much time had passed since he was last in Courtly City. How much time had he been in Brio? How long had he been here, in this place?

He was looking in one direction as he stepped in another, only to find that his foot was firmly stuck in a swampy mud patch.

When he tried to pull his foot up, it became tangled by roots. He pulled as hard as he could and then felt a searing pain in his ankle. He felt himself start to sink.

Frantically searching around, he grabbed onto some vegetation and was able to pull his body onto more firm land. With much arduous work, he finally extracted his wounded ankle from the thick mud.

With only his hand, he cleared away the remaining mud from his foot. He concluded puddles like these must indicate dangerously swampy territory. He would have to make an effort to avoid those.

Trying to stand, Bjorn found that putting weight on that leg was painful, but he was determined to continue moving forward. He had to find something. Shelter. Food. A person. Something.

He couldn't simply stay there. The speed of his progress would be diminished, but he was determined to get away from this area. After some time,Bjorn realized he was pushing himself past the point of exhaustion.

He needed something for energy. He knelt down and tried to eat part of a plant, several of which grew around him in the sand. It tasted bitter. Its blades were sharp against his tongue.

He searched for signs of a path, but he was a city-born creature and knew nothing of survival.

Then he collapsed, no longer able to stand. His ankle throbbing. His hands cut. His belly empty. His energy depleted. Even breathing became a labored effort.

Bjorn rolled onto his back and marveled at the amazing variety of birds, the sounds of which he had never heard in the city.

The plumage of which seemed so foreign and odd, he had no idea so many varieties of birds existed.

Smiling at the irony of being in such a beautiful place, yet fully alone, Bjorn realized that after all he had been through, he could die on this very spot.

Then, he took a deep breath and closed his eyes.

5 CHAPTER 28: (2031) ISLAND: SHORE: BJORN WAKES UP AFTER ISLAND NAP & GETS SLOBBERED

Uncertain how long he had been there, Bjorn Esterday tried to recount to himself the events which led him to this moment.

Back in Courtly City, he had bargained with the editor of the Daily Memo newspaper to cover a story about some smooth-talking con-artist named Watson,

who appealed to anybody who wanted a shortcut to an easier life.

Even during that assignment, Bjorn himself had succumbed to the temptation to take a shortcut.

Using bare minimum effort to cover the Watson story just so he could get the contact information for that new gal he had run into at the train station…What was her name? Something Paradise.

He wondered if the man who stole his identity wasn't also in a hurry to find some shortcut to get out of a tricky situation.

Bjorn shook his head while lying in the sand, surrounded by odd looking plants and long tufts of grass.

Driven by desperate hunger, had he, in ignorance, eaten poison? Was his life quietly slipping away?

Bjorn heard the call of birds, the hum of bees, and the lapping of waves.

If he had chosen to come to this place, it would be a nice vacation spot.

It would be somewhere romantic so he could use his charms on a woman like what's-her-name-Paradise.

But, she was nowhere to be found. No. He was alone.

His desire to shortcut to Teacher Paradise was the choice that had plopped him into Brio, the underwater prison where he had befriended an odd little advocate named Pat Seeds.

Pat, the Brio gardener, had thrown an old fashioned HIB into the escape pod instead of climbing aboard.

Pat Seeds.

Bjorn mused while staring into the sun.

Pat Seeds had displayed more selfless integrity than almost anybody he had ever met in Courtly City.

Pat cared about the other residents of Brio while Bjorn, once again, succumbed to the temptation to shortcut his way out of a painful situation.

His own impetuous actions had hurried along the demise of everybody in Brio...and the biosphere itself.

If he ever told the story about how he had arrived at Brio and how he escaped and why, would anybody believe him?

Would he be lying here now, hungry, exhausted, wounded, if he had followed decent common sense and put forth his very best efforts?

Did his pride make him feel entitled to think he was better than those around him? That the rules didn't apply.

Was he hypocritical by wanting to voice his opinions in the stories he wrote, which pointed out the failings of character in prominent Courtly City personalities?

Was Sammy Scribe right in telling him to take on a lighter tone?

Did Bjorn himself evidence the same characteristics he easily condemned in the people he wrote about in his own articles?

What if Bjorn never covered that story of that obvious con-artist Watson, who sold dreams and timeshares to Atlantis-like underwater villages?

What if Bjorn never took Paradise's information, which his boss, Sammy Scribe, had discovered, in exchange for covering that story?

Where would Bjorn be today if he simply insisted that the Administrators at Sarah Paradise's elementary school tell him to which High School she had been transferred?

Sarah!

That was her first name... Sarah...the last real woman he had met from Courtly City.

Sarah Paradise. Sarah. A woman he

had just met and would probably never see again.

Bjorn sighed as he closed his eyes to shield himself from the bright sun shining high above, suspended in the azure blue heavens.

He inhaled slowly as he lay there amidst razor-sharp tufts of long grass poking up like inviting spear-shaped salads through white sands.

Sarah Paradise was somebody who was more concerned about keeping her word to take some kids on a field trip to Library than her own job, as Sammy Scribe had informed him.

Pat Seeds cared more about the welfare of the residents of Brio than life itself. What did Bjorn care about other than himself?

What cause did Bjorn have? Who- besides himself- did he think about? How could he make the world a better place for...somebody?

Why did he take short cuts and why did they always backfire on him?

Why did he get this chance to breathe surface air when none of the other Brio residents did? Guilt weighed on him, entombing him. He considered the figurative wall created from his hasty actions hurting innocents could only be broken if he dedicated his waking days to doing the right thing.

But, what is the right thing in these days where your only value to your corporation was in how much profit could you make them?

Was he wallowing in self pity? Was this introspection actually even useful, or should he simply say- what is done is done and now move forward? What should Bjorn do? What did he have to go back to in Courtly City? Did he even have a job at the Daily Memo anymore?

Bjorn remained motionless.

Something hot and wet hit his face, startling him.

"Huh?" Bjorn muttered as his shook himself from his guilt-ridden trance of reliving painful images and pondering unhappy memories.

There was that sensation again, but Bjorn couldn't open his eyes. When he tried, his vision was blurred, obscured by some slimy substance, which slowly oozed down his face.

Bjorn barely had time to squeeze his lids shut before being hit again by the impact of a slobbery, panting, heavily pungent blast of breath, which lingered after the deposit of slimy saliva leaked into Bjorn's eyes.

Then, Bjorn heard panting. He felt paws of different sizes climb up onto him.

He was resistant to the idea of becoming somebody's meal and tried to shout, but only a cracking squeak came out of his throat. He tried to move, but his wounded ankle, which had been twisted amongst roots in a swampy pothole, shot blazing pain from his ankle all the way up to his hip.

He could barely move his leg. His arms hit the ground around him, as he tried to grab a stick or something to defend himself in this blind state. He found nothing but blades of grass, which gave him stinging micro cuts has he tried to grab, but failed to uproot the grass.

Unable to find something to clear his eyes, he used the heels of his palms to clean away the vision-obscuring slime, while attempting to prop himself up on one elbow to defend himself against this new foe.

By feel he could tell there was more than one, but how many, he couldn't ascertain. Was Bjorn Esterday about to become somebody's meal...

6 CHAPTER 29: (2031) ISLAND: VILLAGE: LONGFELLOW APOLOGIZES TO THE LOCAL VILLAGE MAN

"Stop it! Stop this instant!"

Furious, Longfellow stomped over to one of his recruits who was having heated words with a villager. The villager, obviously a much older man, was leaning heavily for support against the wall of his shop.

Warren Piece ran to Longfellow and the angry recruit.

Two dogs, Dustin and Austin, trotted rapidly, keeping pace with Longfellow.

Longfellow knelt down to pick up the remnants of a broken cane. He turned to the older man leaning against the wall.

Longfellow calmly asked the man, "Please sir, explain to me what happened."

The recruit interrupted, "I was doing my exercises and he got in the way, the old fool!"

Longfellow spun around and with only a piercing angry gaze, ordered the recruit to stop talking.

Warren Piece arrived breathlessly. He looked back to make sure the other recruits were sitting on the ground where he had ordered them to remain.

"What's going on?" Warren asked as he caught his breath, "I just heard the noise. Shouting."

"I'm trying to find out," Longfellow replied to Warren. The recruit started to speak, again.

Warren put his hand on the boy's shoulder and said, "Remember, you don't speak unless spoken to."

Warren leaned in to whisper to Longfellow, "I think the recruits may be acting up because they found out from somebody in the village that the Twins are arranging a barrier. Gossip has it that the AnCors will get paid, but a bunch of them are in jail in Courtly, so…"

Longfellow whispered back and said, "If it is true, it's just another obstacle. You can assure our young warriors that we will get home. Triumphant."

Warren looked at Longfellow who gave Warren a silent signal to take the recruit away, permitting Longfellow to speak with the old man in private.

"Please sir," Longfellow asked the old man after the recruit and Warren had left, "What happened?"

The old man stammered, "The boys were exercising as I've seen your lot do, but that one," The old man indicated the recruit standing next to Warren, "I suppose you are teaching them how to use a slingshot and he was mixing it with some fancy kicking exercise."

"Sir..."

The old man's erupting emotions spewed, "I was having trouble crossing the street. It is not as easy for me to move around at my age, you know. That street construction. It makes everything more difficult. But the cobblestones need to be repaired. I only came out to tell your boys...your boys...the ones who look to you as an example...your boys... to keep the noise down. He didn't see me, but he did kick my cane, which broke."

"I am so sorry for..."

The old man held up a palm and continued, "Then, I fell back. I did not have a cane to stabilize myself because your boys broke it. As I tried to break my fall, I upset the fruit cart. I yelled. It is my right to yell at such clodish undisciplined rudeness and inconsideration. The fruit is now trampled on and destroyed. It cannot be sold. Then, after all that…then he tells me I got in his way and he tells me it is my fault. No respect! ”

Longfellow shook his head, “I do sincerely apologize, sir. We will buy all the fruit in the cart, be it broken, dropped or still edible. I’ll take it all. Then, I’ll have the recruits fashion you a new cane.”

“Respect. If they want to become respected men, they need discipline, restraint, and practice. They need manners.”

Longfellow agreed, “They will learn respect, sir. We appreciate you allowing us to live in these parts and we want to let all the villagers know we do respect you. Again, my apologies.”

“Fine,” the old man said. “Can you

walk with me across the street to my home? I'll need assistance until I get my cane."

Longfellow helped the old man into his home, and then marched directly to Warren and the recruit.

"You must demonstrate respect to the villagers. We are not training you to become the town bully, but to understand that every skill learned must be tempered with absolute self-control. That was an old man. What if you were up against an opponent who had firearms? Does your attitude make you bullet proof?"

"No, sir," the recruit muttered, now looking down, "But I was doing what I was told. The exercises."

Warren shook his head, "The exercises were meant to take place over there, not in the middle of the street. You branched off from the others."

Longfellow looked him in the eyes,

"Don't blame. Accept responsibility. Nobody asked you to break that man's cane and wreck the fruit cart."

The recruit stammered, "No sir, but it got wrecked because he fell and I scouldn't see into the future to know he was going to fall. I didn't even know he was there."

Longfellow tapped him on his head and said, "You have all your senses right here. You need to be aware of your surroundings. Every single moment. For your own survival. One mistake like that could not only jeopardize your safety, but that of all the others, as well."

Longfellow took a breath and added, "This is why we routinely ask you 'where are you', and not 'how are you'. You should have sensed that old man and known where you were in relation to him."

Longfellow took another deep breath and ordered, "You will sit out for the rest of the day and fashion two new canes for that old man by this evening."

"Two!" The recruit blurted out, "But he only broke one. And we can buy one from a store inland."

"Yes, two," Longfellow quietly replied. "One extra as an apology for the fellow's inconvenience. Mr. Piece will inspect it to ensure it is high quality."

Longfellow strode away across the roadway to the other recruits, who were sitting, expectantly, on the ground. Hushed whispers silenced as soon as Longfellow approached.

Warren and the scolded recruit followed. Longfellow addressed the troops.

"Respect," he started. "We are not bullies like the AnCors."

One muttered something about needing to show strength by not caring what others thing.

Longfellow whipped around to lock eyes with that recruit.

Longfellow took a deep breath and said, "To demonstrate strength, we need discernment to judge when to unleash our power and when to contain it. To obtain trust and admiration, we must earn respect. To earn respect we must show others that we care about their well being. Do you understand we are here...training...away from the bullies of the Twins who forced themselves into AromaX, our home? Do you understand we will beat the Twins but not by devolving into their tactics?"

"Sir. Yes, sir. "

Longfellow continued, "I want everybody to get it. We do not force our will onto the locals like the Twins. We need to demonstrate daily in our small actions that we can live harmoniously and respectfully with these villagers. Do you all understand?"

The group of recruits agreed, "Yes, sir."

Longfellow glanced at the ground and then up into the sky. Then his eyes skimmed over the emotionless faces of his recruits as he continued with measured tones, "That means, if you see a villager who needs help, help."

"Help. Yes, sir." They replied in unison.

Longfellow advised, "If you accidentally break something, replace it with twice what they lost."

"Twice. Yes. Sir." The recruits repeated.

Longfellow reminded, "Be polite. We need the locals to welcome us here because we don't know how long we can remain here safely. Remember, any new skills you learn are intended to help the unit as a whole, not for you to show off and then upset the fruit cart. We must pool our skills so we can strategically overcome the crass bullying crude tactics of the Twins and their soulless brainwashed devotees. We are better than that."

Warren looked behind him at all the mess created by the overturned cart. Longfellow caught the glance and then turned back to the seated recruits.

Longfellow continued with his lecture, "When one of us fails, it hurts us all. We need to remind each other to follow the rules. To keep each other sharp and safe. Tonight and for however long it lasts, every meal will be that fruit. Stand up."

Warren Piece made the motion for the recruits to stand to their feet. They stood at attention, all eyes on Longfellow.

Longfellow announced, "Exercises for the day have been canceled. Instead, we will all pick up that fruit, straighten the cart up and wheel it back to the storefront where it had been."

He continued smoothly, "Carry all the fruit, smashed or whole, back to our kitchen, where we will prepare it for dinner or bury it in the back."

Next, he put his hand on the shoulder of the offending recruit, "During our recreation time, this one will be in the shed whittling a couple of new canes to replace the one he broke. Questions?"

One recruit raised her hand. "Um, is this just for today or...I mean I don't think in AromaX..."

Longfellow interrupted, "Not every recruit here was born in AromaX. We are not replicating the laws of AromaX here, but we are making our own much improved, more effective rules and regulations. We must be better people than we were in our home world. We must be better,"

He took a deep breath. "Generations ago, my family came from Canada, yet eventually we moved to AromaX. Where was I from?"

"Canada, sir."

"We do not follow rules simply because they are tied to a geography. We follow our present, productively appropriate rules because we have learned by hard experience that doing what is objectively right it is the right thing to do. Understood?"

"Right thing. Understood, sir."

Longfellow concluded with, "We want the villagers to willingly want to have us around. Because us being here makes their lives better. Are we clear?"

The troops nodded, "Clear, sir."

Then Longfellow clapped his hands twice and said, "Now! We clean up."

Longfellow and Warren looked to the house where the old man had been helped.

The old man had his window open and was watching the entire interchange.

He nodded to Longfellow and Warren Piece. The old man was satisfied that the matter was being handled with professionalism.

Longfellow glanced around. Others in the village were quietly observing how Longfellow was handling the matter.

By the expressions on their faces, the locals were satisfied that this mistake would not happen again. They were convinced this incident would serve as a lesson to all the recruits and that they would all understand the importance of respect.

But would the villagers ever believe that they are better off with these AromaX immigrants? Would they welcome these trainees?

7 CHAPTER: What Just Happened?

In the year 2031, Sarah Paradise went on two blind dates, both set up by her fellow teacher, Georgia Peach. Sarah decides not to go out again with either of these men, and she is no longer going to accept future date-offers from Georgia.

Sarah introduces Georgia to Mrs. Libris, the librarian.

Bjorn Esterday is washed ashore, exhausted, and is greeted by the slobbering licks of a dog.

While out in the village with his recruits, Longfellow admonishes what should be learned from the way a local resident had been treated.

Longfellow used the fruit cart incident to teach all the recruits that character matters. They can use strategy, and their limited resources to combat the crude power of the bully tactics which forcibly took over AromaX.

Warren and Longfellow both have a dream of not just welcoming AromaX refugees, but of training them so that one day they can take back AromaX.

Longfellow used the situation to teach his team the meaning of true respect.

Warren Piece, also a former resident of AromaX, aids Longfellow in grooming the recruits. He wants to teach them all to be better than they were. But, will it be enough to overcome the odds.

8 Did You Know

The region of Maastricht in the Netherlands, is home to a variety of vineyard. Some were planted back in the Roman times.

They produce varieties such as Pinot Noir, Müller-Thürgau, and Riesling. The Dutch climate, however makes it more of a challenge to produce other types of vines, so these grape varieties are cultivated in very small batches using Merlot and Cabernet Sauvignon grapes.

Some say the Romans who settled in the Netherlands first planted crops in Maastricht, called Traiectum ad Mosam as far back as the year 968 AD.

9 Vocabulary

This fictional series introduces some terms unique to the modern world. Also used are standard terms which we encourage you to investigate in a dictionary for your own edification. A consolidated full list of vocabulary for all GONE books is located in the Conversation Station supplemental book.

Casanova A Fictional character with the reputation to influence and charm women.

HTTYM This is an acronym for a book titled "How to Troubleshoot Your Mate", a book created as if it were a software troubleshooting manual to smooth out problems with your romantic other half.

Comm   This is the device used by residents in Courtly City to communicate on the Courtly network. It acts as a cellular telephone. The word was truncated from "communication".

With a cellular telephone, one person can call another user even if they have a different service provider.

To maintain control over the communications of corporation city residents, the Comm only allows people of one corporate city to communicate on the comm with other users who also have a comm provided by that specific corporation city.

ABOUT Wynter Sommers

Wynter Sommers is the pseudonym for an American writing team, which harnesses multiple skills in technology, research, history and education. Formally trained with a PhD in Education, Wynter Sommers blends academic classroom experience, with corporate sophistication, and a passion for developing more effective student insights through engaging storytelling.

Wynter Sommers has a heart to inspire creativity and develop critical thinking skills, all to encourage readers to make wise choices in life.

Wynter Sommers takes each story and weaves the plot with classic gripping elements, which endure throughout repeated readings, revealing new meanings each time the story is explored. The small choices a reader makes in real life could have a lasting effect in future generations. This set of stories shows the origin of not just Bjorn Esterday and Sarah Paradise, but of their ancestors and the sort of world which was established, which unfolded in each generation until Bjorn and Sarah met.

It is rewarding to learn of heartfelt, thought provoking conversations taking place globally about the characters of these books. Should the reader be presented with extraordinary circumstances, it is the sincerest wish that they act with honor, truth and integrity to overcome obstacles in real life whilst the reader hones skills of self-reliance and collaborative teamwork despite barriers outside of the reader's control. Wynter Sommers hopes you enjoy the other ***Bjorn Esterday Was not Born Yesterday*** stories in this series.